10. A Whale of a Time

"I thought Vikings were supposed to wear horned helmets," gasped Anil, sagging under the weight of an iron bell.

"The only place you'll see them is in comics," Worm told him before he and Dazza were bundled away at knifepoint towards the abbey entrance.

"Oh God! We're not gonna have to go in there, are we?" cried Dazza. "We'll be burnt alive!"

"It's either that or be stabbed to death," Worm shouted as they were separated. "Try and cover your face with something. Just grab the nearest thing you find and get back out fast."

Join the Time Rangers on tour!

In the Peak District:

In the Cotswolds:

In London:

Northwards:

TIME RANGERS

10. A Whale of a Time

Rob Childs

DAZZA
GOALKEEPER – 1

WORM
RIGHT-BACK – 2

STOPPER
CENTRE-BACK – 5

RAKESH
RIGHT-MIDFIELD – 4

MR STOPPARD
MANAGER

JACKO
CENTRE-MIDFIELD – 8

SPEEDIE
RIGHT-WINGER – 7

RYAN
CENTRE-FORWARD – 9

ANIL
LEFT-WINGER – 11

MR THOMAS
MANAGER

For my wife Joy, with special thanks

Scholastic Children's Books,
Commonwealth House,
1-19 New Oxford Street,
London WC1A 1NU, UK
A division of Scholastic Ltd
London ~ New York ~ Toronto ~ Sydney ~ Auckland
Mexico City ~ New Delhi ~ Hong Kong

First published in the UK by Scholastic Ltd, 1999

Copyright © Rob Childs, 1999
Cover illustration copyright © Simon Dewey, 1999
Inside illustrations copyright © David Kearney, 1999

ISBN 0 439 01184 1

Typeset by
Cambrian Typesetters, Frimley, Camberley, Surrey
Printed by
Cox and Wyman Ltd, Reading, Berks

10 9 8 7 6 5 4 3 2 1

1 Goal!

"What a view!" exclaimed Mr Thomas, gazing over the harbour towards the abbey ruins high on the opposite cliff. "One of my favourite places, Whitby. We've had some good times here in years gone by, eh, Ryan?"

"Yes, Dad," he replied dutifully, aware of the smirks from a few of his teammates. They'd also had experiences of times in the past – good and bad.

"Boat trips out to sea, spot of fishing..." continued the manager of

Tanfield Rangers wistfully "...messing about in rock pools down the coast at Robin Hood's Bay."

Worm pricked up his ears. "Robin Hood's Bay?" he repeated.

Mr Thomas grinned. "Thought even you must've had enough of that old outlaw by now, Michael. You've hardly stopped talking about him since we left Sherwood Forest on Sunday."

Worm was about to say something else when Ryan dug him in the ribs with his bony elbow. It was a well-disguised blow by the team's leading scorer, normally delivered as a warning to any defender who was marking him too tightly, but Worm's bright orange anorak softened the impact.

The Rangers were all well wrapped up to keep out the biting gusts of wind that swirled in off the North Sea. It was almost cold enough to make the nearby statue of Captain Cook shiver. Their co-manager, Mr Stoppard, attempted to give the boys a potted biography of the famous explorer, an unwise decision when his own maritime knowledge was about as shaky as one of the sea captain's ships in a storm.

"Now, as you may know," he began, "Captain James Cook sailed the southern oceans and discovered Australia in ... um..."

"1770," said Worm helpfully, loading a new film into his camera.

"Yes, quite right – just testing. He set out from Whitby on his first voyage in a ship called the ... um..."

"*Endeavour.*"

Mr Stoppard gave up. He realized he should have known better than to try to compete with Rangers' travelling historian. Worm was revelling in their half-term tour. Most of the previous day had been spent in York, walking the city's Roman walls and visiting the Viking Centre, before they headed further north for the next match.

The under-thirteen footballers were restless now, eager to get back into soccer action. While Worm clicked away at the statue, the other players drifted towards an archway made from a pair of huge jawbones, a memorial to Whitby's prosperous whaling industry two hundred years ago. Ryan was dribbling a football along as usual and the target proved irresistible. Driven low and hard,

10

the ball smacked into one side of the arch and spun off down the path that led to it.

"Goal!" he cried. "In off the post – the winner!"

"Grow up, Ryan," snapped Mr Thomas, unimpressed with his son's marksmanship. "Show some respect for once, will you?"

"Soz, Dad, I always shoot through this arch," Ryan grinned. "Scored a hat trick on our last holiday."

"Aye, well, make sure you score another one this afternoon against the Whitby Whalers – in proper goals."

Worm arrived on the scene and was just about to walk underneath the archway when the team's goalkeeper grabbed him by the arm.

"Oh, no, you don't," said Dazza. "It looks too much like one of your so-called time gates to me. If we let you waltz through there, you'll probably pitch up on a whaling ship in the middle of the Arctic Ocean – and drag us with you as well."

"Don't talk rubbish," Worm retorted, pulling a face. "Nothing happened in York, did it?"

"No, you must be losing your magic touch," teased Anil, Rangers' lanky left-winger. "Perhaps it's wearing off at last."

Mr Thomas cut across them. "We promised you some free time this morning, lads, but don't get up to any mischief, OK?" he warned. "Meet back here at the whalebone arch by twelve noon. We're going to treat you all to a delicious meal of freshly caught cod."

The managers divided the squad into fours by the simple method of pointing at players standing near one another. To their dismay, Ryan and Dazza found themselves lumbered with Worm, plus Anil.

"Make sure you stay in your groups. Nobody is to go wandering off on their own," said Mr Stoppard, looking directly at Worm. "I've no idea where you get to, Michael, but we seem to spend half our time searching for you on these trips."

Everyone laughed as Worm reddened. "You're responsible for him, Ryan, right?" said his dad. "Don't go losing him anywhere."

"Oh, thanks," Ryan muttered under his breath. "*Anywhere* is just about where we're likely to end up with Worm for company."

2 Fire!

Four hooded figures leant over the bridge that spanned the mouth of the River Esk, staring down at the empty fishing boats moored by the quayside. The windswept scene at low tide was as bleak as their mood.

"So what are we going to do now?" asked Anil.

"Dunno," said Dazza. "Better ask the Whitby expert here."

Ryan scowled. "Shown you all the places I'm interested in."

"Oh, yeah, fascinating," said Worm sarcastically. "Two amusement arcades and your favourite café. They wouldn't even let us in on our own."

"Well, the other things are closed, ain't they? It's late October – not exactly the height of the tourist season, y'know."

Worm was sulking. The others kept refusing his requests to visit the ruined abbey. "C'mon, we've still got another hour to kill," he whined, trying again. "Anything's better than just standing here, freezing to death."

"What, slogging up 199 steps to get up the cliff?" scoffed Ryan. "Sure!"

"Look, I only want to take a couple of photos. No harm in that, is there? Then when we come back down it'll be time for lunch."

Thoughts of a hot meal cheered them up a little. "OK, Worm, you win," conceded Dazza reluctantly. "But just keep your distance from the abbey. We don't trust you. No going through any door or archway in the walls – or anything else that looks like it might play time-tricks on us, right?"

Worm beamed, pleased to have got his own way for a change. "Did you know that some of the *Dracula* story was set near the abbey?" he said as they crossed the swing bridge into the old side of town. "The vampire lurked around the church graveyard up there for a while."

"Worm wants to star in a horror movie now – *The Time Rangers Meet Dracula*!" laughed Anil. "Good job for us he's only a fictional character."

"Yeah, that's what we thought about Robin Hood, too," Ryan muttered. He stuffed the football inside the front of his coat and trudged behind the others, hands in pockets, along the narrow, almost deserted streets.

Anil glanced round at him and chuckled. "You look as if you're pregnant!"

"Couldn't care less what I look like. My hands were dropping off."

By the time they arrived at the bottom of the ancient flight of stone steps, rain was beginning to fall from an ominously darkening sky.

"This is ridiculous," Ryan stated. "What's the point of going right up there in this weather? It'll be blowing a monster gale higher up."

It was too late. Worm was already bounding up the wide curving stairway and he pretended not to hear his team-mates' cries, almost drowned in the wind, to come back down.

"It's no good, we'll have to follow him," said Dazza. "We can't afford to let him out of our sight. Your dad will do his nut if we go back without him."

Ryan groaned. "Typical of Worm, this is. If he gets us into any more trouble, I'll kill him."

"He has saved your life a couple of times," Anil felt bound to point out.

"Oh, yeah – like when, for instance?"

"Like when the Romans were going to feed you to the lions."

"Well, OK, maybe that once," Ryan admitted with a shrug. "But if it weren't for him messing about with time, I wouldn't have been in danger of becoming cat food in the first place!"

They started up the steps themselves, taking them two at a time until their legs quickly tired. They pulled their hoods tighter to shut out the stinging rain, aware only of the seemingly endless steps beneath their feet and the sound of their own heavy breathing.

When they eventually reached the top of the cliff, Ryan began to feel a little light-headed. He peered up and noticed a red glow in the sky. Puzzled, he had an uneasy sensation that things were not at all as they should be. "What the hell's going on?" he murmured. "Where's St Mary's Church?"

Oblivious to any changes, Dazza had caught up with Worm who had come to a transfixed halt. "It's stupid going any further," the goalkeeper shouted above the wind. "We're getting soaked. C'mon, back down."

"Look, look! Can't you see?" Worm yelled. "The abbey's on fire!"

The boys stood rooted to the spot in confusion, trying to make sense of the nightmarish scene in front of their eyes. Several seconds passed before they realized they weren't staring at the towering ruins of the medieval abbey. The burning buildings ahead of them were small and squat. Their attention was also distracted by the fleeing, robed figures – nuns as well as monks – some hurling themselves or being thrown, screaming, off the cliff.

Anil suddenly cried out in alarm. "The steps have vanished! There's no way back down. We're trapped."

"So where are we this time, Worm?" Dazza demanded. "C'mon, you must know. You've brought us here."

Worm ignored the accusation. "This must be the original Saxon abbey built in the seventh century by Saint Hilda," he told them. "Dead important place it was – they even fixed the date of Easter here."

"What happened to it?"

"This…" Worm said simply. "It got destroyed in the year 867."

"Who by?"

There was no need for Worm to supply the answer to that question.

A group of men brandishing swords and axes was rushing towards them, long hair flowing out from beneath their metal helmets. After the Rangers' visit to the Jorvik Centre in York, all four boys knew instinctively what these men were.

Worm decided it wouldn't be worth asking if they might care to pose for his camera. He didn't know the Viking equivalent of "Say cheese"!

3 Vikings!

The language barrier was not a problem. The point of a sword at your throat has meant pretty much the same thing throughout the ages:

One false move and you're dead!

It was a total lack of movement on their part that probably saved the lives of the four time travellers. Sheer panic had blocked out any thoughts of trying to run away.

"Just don't do anything stupid," hissed Worm out of the corner of his mouth as the Vikings surrounded them, eyeing their strange clothing with mild curiosity.

"Like following you up them steps, you mean," muttered Ryan, wincing as one of the men leered at him and prodded his bulging coat with a sword.

The warriors then seemed to lose interest in their new captives and shoved them along a muddy track towards the Saxon abbey. Its small stone church was being plundered as it burned. Terrified monks and nuns were forced into the flames to fetch out anything of value, while others were made to carry off the goods under guard.

"Guess they needed a few extra slaves," grunted Ryan as a coarse bulky sack was thrust into his arms.

"I thought Vikings were supposed to wear horned helmets," gasped Anil, sagging under the weight of an iron bell.

"The only place you'll see them is in comics," Worm told him before he and Dazza were bundled away at knifepoint towards the abbey entrance.

"Oh God! We're not gonna have to go in there, are we?" cried Dazza. "We'll be burnt alive!"

"It's either that or be stabbed to death," Worm shouted as they were separated. "Try and cover your face with something. Just grab the nearest thing you find and get back out fast."

Worm whipped his scarf off and tied it over his mouth, but the heat inside the building was almost unbearable. He couldn't see anything at first. The smoke was too thick and his eyes stung so much, it felt as if they were being fried like a couple of eggs. He tripped over something lying on the floor and toppled forwards across the flagstones.

"Not quite so bad down here," he murmured, then saw that he'd fallen over the motionless body of a nun. Her hair was sizzling.

Worm crawled frantically away,

gagging into his scarf at the smell of charred flesh, until his hands made contact with a small hard object. He paused to check what it was, if only to take his mind off the dead woman.

"Some sort of bead necklace with a cross on it," he decided, slipping it into a pocket of his anorak for safe keeping.

He squinted around the smoke-filled interior and realized he must be near the altar. "Got to find something bigger so at least it looks like I've been trying ... this'll have to do."

It was a large chair with carved armrests and he staggered along with it behind a limping, hooded monk who clearly knew the best route to take. Once outside, Worm knelt on the wet ground, heaving and retching as he gulped in lungfuls of air. It tasted so sweet.

His relief, however, was short-lived. Almost immediately a Viking hauled Worm up and flung him roughly back into the abbey. He'd lost his scarf somewhere, but stuffed a handkerchief to his face instead to prevent himself breathing in too much smoke. He sank down again to floor level and made out a figure slumped on some steps just ahead.

"Dazza! Is that you?"

A low groan came back in response. Worm scurried over to him and pulled down Dazza's fur-lined hood that was starting to smoulder.

"C'mon, you can't stay here, we've gotta get you outside," he choked, helping Dazza to sit up. "And this thing too. We can't go out empty-handed."

Dazza had managed to drag a wooden chest to the steps before being overcome by the effects of smoke, but Worm found it too heavy and awkward to lift on his own. "C'mon, Dazza, it's not far," he urged. "We can do it."

The short journey seemed to last for ever. Worm had to slide the chest most of the way, as well as providing support for the groggy Dazza. Part of the roof suddenly crashed down nearby in a shower of flames and debris, sparking their instincts of self-preservation enough to make a final uncoordinated surge for the door together.

They made it outside just in time before the arched doorway itself cracked and collapsed behind them. The boys lay sprawled on the grass, semi-conscious, while a warrior smashed open the chest's metal lock with his axe to examine its contents. He broke into a wide grin of delight on seeing the treasure of coins, silver plates and precious ornaments.

The man kicked Worm and Dazza until they struggled to their feet, fearing they were going to be sent back inside to certain death, but he now had other plans for them. Indicating his orders by waving his axe first at the chest and then towards the cliff, his meaning finally registered on the boys' dulled senses.

The wind and rain had revived Dazza sufficiently for him to be able to take his share of the load and they stumbled off with the chest, glad to be going away from the blazing abbey.

Dazza coughed and spluttered in an effort to find his voice. "Thanks for what you did in there," he croaked. "I'd never have got out by myself."

"Just wish you'd picked something lighter," Worm grunted by way of a reply. "This weighs a ton."

They caught each other's eye and there was no need for either of them to say anything more.

The two Rangers joined a trail of people who were being herded towards the edge of the cliff, where screeching gulls added their noise to the howling wind and the roar of the flames. There was a path of sorts snaking downwards, but it would have been a hazardous descent at the best of times.

And this, most definitely, was not one of those.

4 Help!

"Didn't know if we'd ever see you again."

Worm and Dazza whirled round at the unexpected sound of Ryan's voice behind them. "Likewise," Worm replied, his teeth gleaming white in his smoke-blackened face.

"We thought you'd had it when you went into the abbey," said Anil. "We never saw you come back out."

"I nearly didn't," Dazza admitted. "If it hadn't been for—"

Worm cut in. "What have you two been doing, anyway?"

"This is our second trip down the cliff," said Ryan. "Watch how you go, it's dead slippery. Some people have finished up on the rocks below."

They soon saw what he meant when they began the treacherous descent. Each shaky step had the potential to be their last. The boys' only advantage was that their stronger footwear helped them to get a better grip on the steep muddy track than the monks' sandals. Conditions were made even worse by the battering they received on the exposed cliff from the wind.

"Reckon there's a big storm brewing," said Ryan during a brief hold-up when somebody dropped his burden down the cliff face. A Viking took swift retribution for the loss by making sure that the poor monk followed it.

"Wonder if they're going to risk putting to sea," said Worm.

"Dunno, but they've got a whole fleet of ships waiting – look."

Worm stared down for the first time and saw two of the Viking longships had been drawn up on to the shore. He could also see that some of the captives were being hauled aboard the ships along with the looted cargo.

"Looks like they're taking passengers too," he pointed out.

"Oh no!" wailed Anil. "I always get seasick!"

"That'll be the least of our problems," groaned Dazza, feeling nauseous already from vertigo. "Bet they'll throw us overboard."

Worm shook his head. "We'll probably still be of some use to them when they get home, carrying stuff and that," he said before adding, "then they'll kill us."

Dazza suffered a dizzy spell as they moved on again and his left foot slipped from underneath him, almost yanking Worm off-balance too. Only the weight of the chest itself saved them. It plopped into the mud and stuck fast, wedged against a tree root sticking out of the cliff. Both boys clung on to the chest for dear life until Anil and Ryan helped them to stand up. It had been a stomach-churning, heart-stopping few moments for everyone.

Reaching the bottom slowly without further mishap, the Rangers worked to load one of the ships with the spoils of victory. They had no time to admire the sleek craft with its decorative shields attached along the sides and a carved figurehead of a wolf on the arched bow. They climbed into the stern and slumped uncomfortably among the sacks and boxes as more of the warriors returned from the pillage on the cliff top. The incoming tide refloated the ship and the oarsmen pulled together powerfully to propel it out to sea into the teeth of the gale.

"Surprised we don't have to do all the rowing as well," Ryan muttered.

Worm was considering whether he might risk trying to get some photos of the Vikings. He'd never had his camera with him before on a time adventure to prove where they'd been, and this seemed too good a chance to miss. Photographs of real Viking longships filled with treasure!

He waited until they were many miles out into the North Sea before taking the small camera from one of the deep pockets of his anorak. The sea was so rough, however, it made lining up a shot very difficult. From being on top of a wave, the ship would lurch down into a hollow to douse them with cold water.

"Just have to trust to luck and see if anything turns out," Worm decided. "Here goes."

Squirming between his teammates to seek different views, he reeled off a dozen snaps in quick succession. But his efforts did not go unnoticed.

"Watch it!" cried Ryan. "I think that guy up the front has seen you. I don't reckon he likes you pointing something at him."

The warrior began to pick his way between the rowers, taking a knife from his belt as he approached the Rangers. But his attention was caught by a warning shout from one of the other men. The ship nearest to them had overturned in the storm, spilling its contents and crew into the sea.

The helmsman tried to steer towards the stricken ship, but failed to get close enough to make a rescue attempt. And soon they found themselves in trouble too. The square sail was suddenly ripped into shreds, the mast snapped and the ship was flung on to its side as a huge wave crashed over it.

The Rangers were pitched headlong into the shockingly cold water. Numbed to the bone, they were only vaguely aware of other bodies around them and flotsam from the ship that was breaking up and sinking.

"Oh, God, this is it!" cried Dazza

before he was sucked under as well. "We've really had it this time."

The water closed over his head and everything went black.

Out of the mist sailed a three-masted whaling ship, the *Resolution*, returning home after months away in the icy waters around Greenland. Two of the crew were perched high in the rigging, lashing a pair of whale jawbones to the forward mast to signal the success of their trip. The hold was full of blubber.

The Time Rangers saw none of this. They were too busy drowning.

It was just as well for them, therefore, that one of these men spied something bright orange bobbing in the sea off the port side. He peered through the swirling haar that enveloped the ship and gave a loud cry.

"Man overboard!"

Several crew members on the deck below ran to the port rail. "There 'e be!" shouted one, pointing.

"There's two of 'em!" exclaimed another. "Nay, more – look!"

The ship's captain emerged from his cabin and took charge of the situation. "Lower a boat," he ordered. "Go and bring them aboard."

"Aye, aye, Cap'n Scoresby, sir."

"What if they be dead, sir?"

"Then we'll give them a proper Christian burial at sea," he replied.

One of the small harpoon boats was lowered over the side and rowed towards the area where the bodies had been sighted. The harpooneer was standing in the bows and picked out four shapes in the water. There was no sign of life. "Ah reckon they be gonners a'ready," he sighed. "Nowt we can do for them poor souls."

At that moment, the orange-coated

figure lifted his head and managed to raise an arm and give a weak wave. It was the first indication that the rescue attempt might not be too late.

Each boy in turn was lifted into the boat where they lay, barely moving, like beached whales. Ryan was the first to stir, still hugging the football that had helped to keep him and Dazza afloat. "Where are we?" he groaned.

"Middle o' nowhere, young fellow," answered the harpooneer. "You ain't got no right still to be alive, I tell yer. Where's yer ship?"

"Bottom of the sea by now, I guess. We got shipwrecked in a storm."

"Ain't bin no storm in these parts. The sea's flat calm."

"But the Vikings..."

The man guffawed. "Vikings! Ah reckon your brain's got waterlogged, m'lad. Ain't bin no Vikings round 'ere for nigh on a thousand year!"

Worm sat up with a jolt and spat out a mouthful of saltwater. He looked around, trying to take in his new surroundings. "It's gone," he said miserably.

"What has?" asked Ryan.

"My camera. Must've lost it when we hit the water."

Ryan gave a shrug. "Just as well maybe. Pictures of Vikings would've taken some explaining at the chemist's when you got 'em developed."

5 Banned!

"Uugh!" spluttered Ryan, pulling a face. "What *is* this stuff?"

The four survivors had been taken to the captain's cabin, where they were stripped of their wet clothes and wrapped in layers of blankets. Strong, hot drinks were also tipped down their throats and coursed through their shivering bodies like molten lava.

Worm grinned. "Best not to ask. Just make it look like you're better so they don't give you another one."

"How did you and Anil stay afloat?"

"Luck. We were holding on to a

couple of sacks and they must've had some air trapped inside them."

"D'yer think all the Vikings drowned?"

"Well, they certainly didn't pass through the time gate with us."

"A time gate in the sea?"

"Why not? Trouble is, we seem to have come through it too early," Worm sighed. "By the smell of it, I'd say this is an old whaling ship..."

He broke off, suddenly aware that someone else was listening. A youth of about their own age was crouching nearby, staring at them, his long dark hair tied back behind his head. "Are you the cabin boy?" Worm said, wondering how much he'd understood of the conversation.

"I'm Will Scoresby and my pa's the captain – the best whaler in the world," he replied proudly. "And I'm going to grow up to be just like him."

Worm didn't doubt it. He'd read a booklet in the hostel about Whitby's famous whaling family, the Scoresbys. The captain himself entered at that moment, a big muscular man who seemed to fill the cabin with his bulk.

"I'm glad you don't seem too much the worse for your ordeal," he said after checking the state of their health. "You've had a remarkable escape."

"Were we spotted from the crow's-nest?" asked Worm, then hesitated as the captain appeared puzzled. He knew that Captain Scoresby had invented the small look-out platform on top of a mast, but realized he might have jumped the gun, chronologically speaking.

"I mean, I saw you had someone up high, giving him a sort of bird's eye view over the sea," he rambled on, "and ... um ... I just thought it was a bit like a nest up a tree ... kind of thing, y'know..."

Worm tailed off, but the notion had taken root in the captain's mind. "Hmm, *crow's-nest*. Quite like the sound of that, m'boy..." he said, stroking his beard. "Now then, I don't know what the four of you were doing right out at sea on your own, but if you enjoy adventure, there're jobs for you all on my ship when you're older – sailing the oceans hunting whales."

The boys exchanged furtive glances but didn't respond to the offer until the captain left.

"Don't much fancy that as a future career," murmured Dazza.

"Dead right there," Ryan agreed. "I wanna be a pro footballer, not a lousy whaler!"

Will Scoresby spoke up, outraged. "Whaling is noble work. It needs great courage."

"It's also cruel," Ryan retorted.

Will looked blank. "Cruel? What do

you mean? They are just whales. Who cares about whales?"

"We do," Anil insisted, sitting up for the first time. "You shouldn't kill whales. It's wrong. They're in danger of extinction because of people like you."

"There are millions of whales. The sea is full of them," he scoffed. "Besides, we need the oil to burn in our lamps."

"Oil lamps! It's about time you got up to date, mate," Ryan mocked him. "You've never even heard of electricity, have you? You know nothing about computers, cars, aeroplanes, spaceships..."

Ryan was in danger of getting completely carried away. "Belt up!" Worm snapped. "You can't go shooting your mouth off like that. Remember where we are."

"Oh, don't worry, I know where we

are. In the right place at the wrong time as usual – all thanks to you."

"Sure about that?" Worm said pointedly. "You realize there's only two of us Rangers now who've been involved in every time slip – me and you!"

The fishing port of Whitby could be smelt long before the ship reached the harbour. The boiler houses on the quayside were busy extracting the valuable oil from the latest cargo of whale blubber.

The *Resolution* received a rapturous welcome and the work of unloading the barrels of blubber and whalebone began immediately. Nobody caught more whales than Captain Scoresby – especially when he developed the idea of the crow's-nest!

The Rangers spent the night in the captain's house, sharing Will's room, and benefited from a long, if troubled

sleep. Anil seemed to have suffered the worst in the sea and bouts of coughing kept waking him up from his nightmares of marauding Vikings and shipwrecks.

By late morning, wearing their own dried clothes, they felt ready to venture out and wandered down towards the harbour. The whole area reeked of boiling blubber.

"What a stench!" exclaimed Dazza.

"Suppose you get used to it after a while," said Worm.

"Hope we don't have to," muttered Ryan, dribbling the ball along a cobbled alley. "Sooner we find another one of them time gates, the better – so long as we don't have to go jumping in the sea again."

They weaved their way among the crates of fish on the messy quayside until they came across Will repairing one of the ship's sails. "Need any help?" Worm said in greeting. "'Fraid we're no good at stitching, though."

"Reckon you'd be no good at anything, lie-abeds," Will said sharply. "I seen your hands. Looks like you ain't done a day's work in your lives."

"We don't need to use our hands," sneered Ryan, taking offence at the criticism. "Watch this for a bit of skill."

Ryan started up one of his much-practised juggling routines, keeping the ball off the ground with his feet, knees and head. Showing off, he counted aloud to twenty-five touches before Will tossed a piece of blubber into his face to make him lose control of the ball – and his temper.

Before he could react, however, Will picked up a long harpoon that lay by his side. "This is what takes real skill," he smirked, brandishing the weapon. "Throwing one of these into a mighty whale in a rough sea before it crushes your boat."

Ryan was smouldering. "OK, then, Will *Junior*. If you're so clever, let's see how good you are with a ball. C'mon, bet you can't do what I did with it."

Will was not one to refuse a challenge. He began to try and keep the ball in the air, but he only had two kicks before it bounced out of reach. He glared round, daring anyone to laugh, and had another go. His next attempt was even worse. Will immediately scooped the ball back over his own head.

"One, I make that – just short of your record," cackled Ryan. "Not as easy as it looks, eh?"

"Be fair – it does take a lot of practice," said Anil.

"This is what I think of your ball and your stupid game," Will cried and suddenly hoofed it away into the middle of the harbour.

For a few moments, as he watched it splash down into the water, Ryan was open-mouthed and speechless. Then he found his voice. "I'm gonna kill you for that," he yelled, launching himself at Will.

They wrestled one another to the ground, rolling into a fishing net that had been spread out to dry, before the other Rangers managed to pull them apart. They both scrambled to their feet, breathing heavily. Blood was dribbling from Ryan's nose and he wiped it away with his coat sleeve.

Worm stood in between them, acting as referee. "Pack it up, the pair of you," he ordered. "There was no need for any of this."

"He started it," Ryan fumed. "What about our ball?"

"And I shall end it too," said Will generously. "I should not have done that. Come, we shall go and get it together."

Ryan followed him down a vertical wooden ladder attached to the harbour wall and stepped into a small boat. The two boys didn't speak as Will rowed towards the ball and manoeuvred the craft into position to allow Ryan to pluck it out of the water.

Once the ball was safely in his arms, Ryan could not resist returning mischievously to the subject of their argument the previous day.

"Whaling is going to be banned one day, y'know," he taunted.

Will shook his head. "I do not believe you."

"Well, not in your lifetime, I admit – but sometime in the future. We know about such things..."

They lapsed back into a brooding silence, staring at one another across a chasm of two centuries. When they reached the ladder, Ryan put one foot on the bottom rung and pressed down firmly on the side of the boat with the other. Will almost lost his balance and as he wobbled, Ryan's elbow did the rest, toppling him overboard into the water.

Ryan threw the ball into Dazza's arms and scampered up the ladder as fast as he could.

"What did you go and do that for?" gasped Worm, appalled.

"Always enjoy rocking the boat,"

Ryan laughed. "I was just doing my bit for the whales, getting a spot of retaliation in first."

They heard a curse from below and saw Will swimming for the ladder.

"We'd better make ourselves scarce, quick," urged Dazza. "C'mon, run, before Ryan finds out what the point of a harpoon feels like."

6 Quits!

While Ryan and Dazza were having a kickabout on the sands, Worm persuaded Anil to explore the ruins of the medieval abbey with him.

"Wish I still had my camera," said Worm as they reached the top of the cliff steps. "There's more of the abbey left now than in our own time. Various bits of it have collapsed over the years. We're lucky to see it like this."

"Oh yeah, dead lucky," wheezed Anil, stopping to rest and cough. "We're only stuck about two hundred years away from home."

Worm ignored the sarcasm. "Even the cliff itself keeps crumbling into the sea," he sighed. "Time always wins in the end."

"Well, we usually seem to give it a good run for its money..."

Anil was interrupted by a cry from somewhere behind St Mary's Church and he instinctively glanced over his shoulder to check that the steps hadn't disappeared again. To his relief, they were still there.

"Perhaps Dracula's prowling about?" he suggested, only half in jest.

"Doubt it. The book's not even been written yet."

When the cry was repeated, the boys located its position and ran towards the edge of the cliff. They peered cautiously over and saw Will Scoresby hanging from a projecting rock just out of reach.

"Help me up," he gasped. "I can't hold on much longer."

Anil immediately went into action. He hauled off his coat and then lay flat out to dangle it down the cliff. "C'mon, Will, grab this," he urged, "and we'll try and drag you up."

Worm gripped his teammate's legs as Anil braced himself against Will's weight. "Pull, Worm – nice and steady."

There was a horrible tearing sound as the coat fabric ripped under the strain, but Will was close enough now for Anil to get a fistful of his woollen jumper. Will was also able to find some purchase for his feet on the rock and scrambled back up to safety.

All three boys lay on the ground for a few minutes, recovering their breath after their exertions and fright. Will's pride had suffered more damage than his body. "Thank you for saving my life," he said sheepishly.

"I reckon that makes us quits," Anil

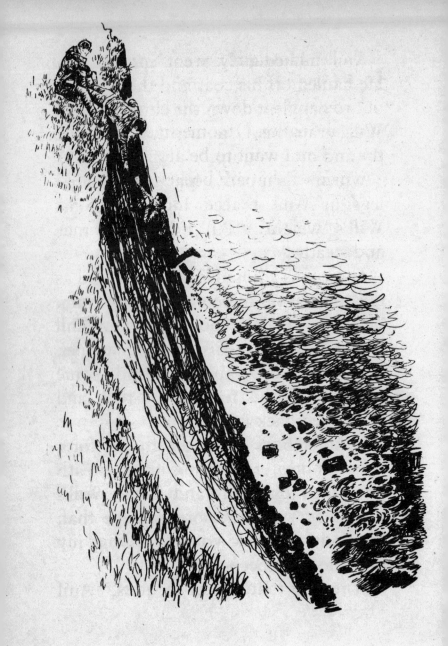

smiled. "How did you get yourself into such a mess?"

"The cliff gave way under a boulder I was sitting on. I sometimes come up here when I want to be alone and think things over that are bothering me."

"Oh, if it's all that stuff that Ryan was spouting, forget it," said Worm, hoping to pass it off. "That's just the way he is."

"It is not only Ryan. You speak of a time gate in the sea and Anil cries out in his sleep about Vikings. Who *are* you people?"

Worm puffed out his cheeks, not quite sure how to answer a question like that. "Well, you're right to be suspicious of us," he admitted. "It's hard to explain – and it must sound pretty crazy – but we're able to travel in time somehow. Maybe we turned up here to save you, I don't know."

Will stared at them with a mixture of

disbelief and fear, almost as if they were supernatural beings. "Only God can decide my destiny," he declared.

"Yes, but fate might need a little helping hand at times. You are destined to do many more things in your life, Will, than catching whales."

Worm suddenly remembered something he had completely forgotten about and unzipped one of the pockets of his anorak.

"What's that?" asked Anil as Worm showed them the necklace of black beads that he'd found in the burning abbey.

"Proof!" Worm exclaimed. "Look, Will, I got to this just before the Vikings did – a thousand years ago! That's how old it is."

"It's beautiful. The beads and cross are made out of jet," he said in wonder. "Whitby is famous all over the world for its jet jewellery."

"Right, and that's why I want you

to have it," Worm said, letting the necklace trickle into Will's lap. "It belongs here, even if we don't."

"I can't take that. People will say I have stolen it."

"Course they won't. Must be so valuable, nobody will be able to claim they own it. Just tell the captain you found it buried near the abbey. He'll know what to do with it for the best."

The temptation was too great. "Only if you promise not to tell Pa what happened to me," he agreed. "He must not learn of my foolishness."

"You couldn't help it if the boulder went crashing down the cliff," said Anil, examining his torn coat ruefully. "You did well not to follow it."

"But I dropped my harpoon."

"Why did you bring that up here?" Anil laughed. "You expect to find a whale waiting for you on top of the cliff? Or are you still looking for Ryan?"

Will pulled a face and stood up. "I must go and find it on the shore or Pa will punish me for losing it."

Worm chuckled as Will ran off towards the steps. "He's just like Ryan with his football. Probably never goes anywhere without that harpoon."

Anil sighed. "If we'd let him fall, it might have saved the lives of a few hundred whales."

"Don't feel too bad about it. Perhaps meeting us lot has had some effect on him. From what I've read, Will turned to writing about animals rather than killing them. He even became a church minister later in life."

"Is that why you gave him the cross?"

"Just seemed the right thing to do," Worm said with a shrug and then grinned. "Besides, can you imagine the questions if I arrived back in the future with a priceless religious relic in my pocket?"

When Worm and Anil eventually returned to the town, they saw Will arguing with their teammates near the harbour.

"Uh-oh – big trouble!" groaned Anil. "Will's got his harpoon back."

They were too late to stop what happened next. Another insult from Ryan gave Will the excuse for exacting revenge for his humiliating ducking.

"C'mon, then, let's see who's the best shot," Ryan dared him. "Me with my football and you with your toy."

Without waiting for an answer, Ryan picked out his target, a ramshackle shed across the street. He tapped the ball forward and let fly, lashing it into the centre of the door and splintering the woodwork.

"Right, beat that!" he smirked, gloating in his success.

"No need. I'll show you who wins between a harpoon and a ball," Will cried and then stabbed down at the ball as it lay in the road at his feet. The sharp metal point instantly pierced the football, which crumpled up and snagged itself on the harpoon's barbs.

Ryan lunged at him in a rage but Will was too quick. He sprinted away across the bridge, ball held up in the air on the end of his harpoon like a lollipop, with Ryan in hot pursuit.

"C'mon, we'll have to go after them," Dazza shouted. "If only to stop Ryan being harpooned as well. We need him for our next match."

Will proved as fast a runner as Speedie, the Rangers right-winger. His pursuers fell further and further behind as they slogged up the slopes of the West Cliff. When they finally got to the top, they glimpsed Will haring off down the other side back towards the town, but there was no sign of Ryan at all.

"Where's he gone to?" panted Anil, coughing again as he caught up. "He's just totally vanished."

They jogged up a trackway, calling out Ryan's name, and then almost ran into the back of him. They could barely believe their eyes. There in front of them stood the rest of the Rangers touring party. Worm spun round and saw that, without realizing, they must have come straight through the site of the whalebone arch and been catapulted back to present-day Whitby.

"About time, too," rasped the voice of Mr Thomas. "Late as usual. I might have known your group would be the last ones to get back."

"And just look at the state of your clothes!" exclaimed Mr Stoppard. "What on earth have you been doing?"

The four time-travellers looked at one another. Their clothes were filthy and torn – and smelled distinctly of fish and boiled blubber.

"Um ... this and that," Ryan stalled, desperately searching for some kind of answer. "Guess you might say we've been having a whale of a time!"

7 Gale!

Anil wasn't fit enough to play against the Whitby Whalers. "Think I've got a cold starting," he told Mr Stoppard after their fish lunch in a harbour café. He'd left most of his meal uneaten.

"Right, best if you try and keep out the wind as much as possible this afternoon," said the manager.

Although it had stopped raining, the wind was still blowing fiercely as the Tanfield party made their way to a local museum to fill the time before the match was due to kick off. It was too cold to hang about outside. There were not even any protests from Ryan, much to his dad's surprise. He'd been to the museum before and took the chance to rest, sprawled across the most comfortable seat he could find.

Jacko pulled up a chair next to him for a while. This was the first time-trip that the Rangers captain had missed and he was eager to find out more details. They hadn't been able to talk openly in the café with the managers sitting nearby.

"Gather you've had a rough time of it," he began.

"Yeah, you could say that. Bet it's the last time anybody will mock me about taking a football everywhere we go."

"So what really happened to the ball? Heard you tell your dad it got kicked into the harbour and floated out to sea."

Ryan grinned. "Well, that was partly true. Didn't think Dad would accept that it got harpooned."

"Harpooned!" Jacko gasped. "Who by?"

Ryan glanced up at a portrait hanging on the wall. "Him!"

Jacko read aloud the inscription underneath the picture. "William Scoresby Junior, Master Mariner (1789–1857)."

"Yeah, but he was no good at football," Ryan grunted.

Anil came up to join them. "See you've caught up with your friend at last," he chuckled, nodding towards the picture. "Worm and me saved his life, you know. He nearly fell off the cliff before he went and burst the ball."

That was the first Ryan had heard about that. "Enough to put anybody in a bad mood, I guess," he sighed.

Worm could have stayed in the museum all afternoon, learning more about Whitby's history. Given a choice between that and playing the match, there would only have been one winner. He was especially interested in the displays devoted to the lives and times of Captain Cook and the Scoresbys, but there was one showcase in particular that he gazed at for ages, lost in thought. The notice next to the polished exhibit read:

Seventh-century jet cross and rosary beads, believed to have belonged once to St Hilda, founder and first abbess of the original Saxon abbey that was destroyed in the Viking raid of AD *867. Presented to William Scoresby Junior in 1803 by unknown travellers.*

"St Hilda's own rosary..." Worm breathed. "Incredible! Wonder if Will ever knew how important it really was?"

In the end, Mr Stoppard had to round

Worm up as everyone else waited in the foyer, ready to leave. "Sorry, time to go," he smiled. "Almost makes you wish you could see Whitby as it used to be in the olden days, eh?"

"I think I've got a pretty good idea what it was like," he murmured in reply.

The cold air hit them like a sledgehammer as soon as they stepped outside the building. And when they arrived at the venue for the game, they found the wind was whistling from one end of the pitch to the other.

"It'll be like playing in a wind tunnel," muttered Mr Thomas. "Which way do you want to kick first if you win the toss, Jacko?"

"Usually prefer to have the wind behind us and try to build up a good lead before half-time," said the captain. "Gives you more confidence to battle it out afterwards."

Ryan butted in. "Nah, best to play into it while you're fresh, I reckon, and then have wind advantage later when both teams are getting knackered."

As it turned out, Jacko had no say in the matter. Scott, the Whalers centre-back and captain, called "Heads!" correctly. "We'll have the wind," he grinned, affecting a loud belch to confirm his decision.

"Suits me – prefer to have it at our backs second half," Jacko lied, trying to hide his own disappointment.

"Huh! We'll be so far ahead by then, you'll need a telescope even to see us."

Worm was already staring hard at one of the opposition. He'd had to do a double-take when he first spotted him, thinking for a moment that they weren't the only ones who had come through the whalebone arch time gate. Worm jogged over to where Anil was sheltering against the changing cabin.

"See that kid with the black hair near the corner flag?" Worm said, pointing him out. "Remind you of anybody?"

Anil peered down the touchline and let out a gasp. "It must be Will's twin brother!"

"Hardly, but I bet they're related. Try and find out his name, will you? We're just about to kick off."

The Rangers soon realized what a tough job they had on their hands as the Whalers swarmed on to the attack in blue-shirted waves. The tourists, playing in their change strip of all-white, could barely get the ball out of their own penalty area at times, never mind clear it over the halfway line.

Anil had a much easier task. Will's double turned out to be one of the substitutes and Anil casually strolled up to stand alongside him on the touch-line. "Hi, you having a good season?" he said to start off a conversation.

The boy shrugged. "So-so. Win some, lose some," he replied and then grinned. "Trouble is, we always seem to lose when I play. They've started to call me Jonah."

"Jonah?"

"Yeah, 'cos they reckon I bring them bad luck. Story of *Jonah and the Whale* in the *Bible* – geddit?"

Anil still looked a little puzzled. "Oh, right, think I've heard it before – not exactly my religion, see."

They were interrupted by an eruption of cheers from the few home supporters who had braved the elements to watch the game. The Whalers had scored. Anil had missed the goal, and it didn't seem as if Dazza had known much about it either. The goalkeeper was standing with his arms outstretched at his sides, the very picture of helplessness.

Anil blew his nose. "Think I'm glad

not to be playing today, er ... sorry, what's your real name?"

"Jon – close enough to being Jonah, I suppose. Must run in the family, this business with whales."

"You're not the one who's descended from the Scoresbys, are you? Only I heard somebody say the Whalers had a Scoresby in the team."

The boy pulled a face. "That's me. Hard to live it down sometimes."

Anil chuckled. "Good name for a footballer as well, though, isn't it? You know, *Scores*-by. Are you a striker?"

"No, 'fraid not. The only goals I tend to score are ones in my own net!"

"No danger of that if you were on the pitch now. I think the only time we've been in your half so far is when we've kicked off."

That fact hadn't escaped Ryan's notice. Even his marker, Scott, had deserted him. He'd gone up to join in the fun around the Rangers penalty box, leaving a couple of other defenders on guard duty near Ryan in the centre-circle.

"C'mon, team," Ryan yelled. "I'm freezing. Give us the ball."

He was under instructions from his dad to stay upfield, just in case Rangers did manage to spring a breakaway raid. Normally he wouldn't have minded letting others do all the work, but it was too cold to stand about doing nothing. Ryan was bursting to get into the action.

When the Whalers won another corner, he dropped back into his own area to help with the marking. The two unemployed defenders looked at each other, wondering what to do, then pushed forward themselves. Even their overweight goalkeeper, looking even fatter under several layers of kit, wandered almost up to the halfway line. He was bored too.

It was Ryan himself who got his head to the ball first, but it was Stopper, the other manager's son, who completed the clearance. He put all his strength into his kick and surprised everyone with the distance he achieved. The ball landed in the empty centre-circle and bounced to the feet of the Whalers goalie just inside his own half.

"Whack it, Blubber," shouted Scott. "Right back up here."

Blubber whacked it as only he could. The ball left his size-nines with the speed and explosive force of a harpoon gun on a modern whaling ship. There was nothing anyone could do but watch the guided missile as it flew through the air, given extra power by the gale behind it.

It looked as though the ball was going

to pass over the crossbar and give Dazza a mile-long trek to fetch it back, but then it swirled and dipped viciously to smack into the net instead. The ball came bouncing back out of the net like a frisky puppy dog and jumped up into Dazza's arms, but it was far too late to claim the catch. Rangers were 2–0 down.

As the celebrating Whalers ran to mob their roly-poly keeper in delight,

Mr Thomas glanced anxiously at his watch. "There's only about ten minutes gone," he groaned. "This could get very embarrassing. How many goals is it going to be by the time we turn round?"

8 Jonah!

The manager need not have been so pessimistic. Rangers defended stubbornly for the rest of the first period and were only trailing by three goals at the interval. And they had even succeeded in scoring one themselves.

In what was virtually their only worthwhile attack of the half, Speedie had dribbled the ball out of defence up the right wing and his pace caught the home side by surprise. Before they could recover and get players back in numbers, he had squared the ball inside to Ryan who fired it low past the Whalers keeper into the net.

"Decided it was no good trying to take the ball round that blubber mountain," Ryan joked as the teams sought a brief, welcome respite from the wind in the changing cabin. "They haven't built the ring road yet!"

"You did well to find any gaps left by that guy," grinned Rakesh, who played behind Speedie in midfield. "It's no wonder they put him in goal – he fills most of it."

"Could be a lot worse, lads," Mr Stoppard told them. "Well battled. Four–one isn't bad in these conditions and that breakaway goal was a real bonus."

"Yeah, when it went in, their captain was totally gobsmacked," laughed Jacko. "He knows it makes their job much harder now into the wind."

"It's their own fault for not making

the most of it," said a relieved Mr Thomas. "Now you go out there second half and show 'em how it should be done. I want to see it raining goals and that big tub of lard in their goal getting drenched."

"Hope 'Jonah' Scoresby comes on," said Anil, telling the others about what the boy had said. "That'd be a good sign for us if he really is a jinx."

"It lets me get a bit of revenge on Will Junior now I know a Scoresby plays for this lot," smirked Ryan, after making sure his dad couldn't overhear. "Better late than never, eh?"

"Pity we can't tell him that we met his ancestors," murmured Worm. "Just think – if we hadn't saved Will's life on the cliff, this kid might never have been born."

The wind seemed to have increased in strength, if anything, when the players went back outside, but the Rangers were caught cold straight from the restart. After the usual tapped kick-off, the ball was swept out wide to the Whalers left-winger, who sprinted past Worm and hooked the ball into the middle. Two defenders got in a tangle with each other, Rakesh miskicked and it was only Stopper's last-ditch, sliding tackle that caused the number nine to blaze his hurried shot over the bar.

Dazza was furious. "Dead sloppy, that was, defence," he yelled. "Sort it out. I don't want to see the ball up this end again."

Dazza's ranting served to re-focus the minds of his teammates and they took the game to the Whalers for the first time in the match. The strong wind was almost as good as having two extra players on the pitch and now it was the Blues' turn to do some desperate defending.

For the first quarter of an hour, however, the Rangers hammered on the door without being allowed in. Every time they found a way through the blockade, they came up against Blubber's formidable barrier. He pushed a shot from Jacko round the post, smothered an awkward skidder from Rakesh, and then a point-blank strike from Speedie bounced off the goalie's vast chest and bobbled away to safety.

But when that defensive dam was finally breached, the floodgates opened. Ryan's well-placed header into the top corner triggered off a cascade of goals, three in seven minutes according to his dad's stopwatch. Speedie's persistence reduced the Whalers' lead to just 4–3, scooping the ball over the line at the second attempt in a goalmouth scramble, and Ryan's hat-trick goal made the scores level.

It was a beauty. Executing a neat one-two pass with Rakesh, Ryan turned with the ball on the edge of the penalty area and thundered a shot with his right foot high into the net. Even Blubber was unable to get his ample body in the way of that screamer.

At that point, the Whalers manager made two substitutions to try and stem the tide, allowing Jon Scoresby to get a taste of the action. It didn't take him long to make his mark on the game.

Unfortunately for him and his team, his earlier prediction to Anil came sadly true. As Speedie's cross speared in from the wing, the defender's attempt to cut the ball out only resulted in a cruel deflection that spiralled over the keeper's head into the net.

"Oh, brilliant! Big help, that is," sneered his captain sarcastically. "Jonah strikes again."

It was almost enough to make Jon wish he *had* never been born. Worm glanced at Anil nearby on the touchline and they exchanged a shrug of mutual sympathy for Will's unlucky descendant.

Anil chuckled to himself softly. "Bet if Jonah had been hunting whales, he'd probably have forgotten to let go of the harpoon."

"C'mon, men, keep this up," cried Jacko. "Don't ease up now just 'cos we're in the lead. We want to score more goals."

Worm swapped places with Dazza for the last five minutes to allow the goalkeeper to run round and warm up a little. After his hectic first-half performance when he had made several crucial saves, Dazza had largely been idle in the second. Worm didn't mind having time on his gloved hands. He spent the rest of the game leaning against the post, musing over their latest adventures. His only regret was that he'd lost his camera.

Dazza threw himself into the fray with great enthusiasm, even on one occasion bursting past Speedie on an overlapping run up the wing. Speedie used him as a decoy and passed the ball inside to his captain instead. Blubber didn't even bother to try and stop Jacko's side-footed curler that clipped the post on its way in. Like many of his teammates now, he had given up the unequal battle against tiredness and the gale.

There can't be many football matches in the history of the game when both goalkeepers have scored, but it happened that afternoon in Whitby. Dazza enjoyed the last word in his own personal duel with Blubber by rounding off a sweeping five-man move with a delicate chip over his stranded counterpart. It was a goal in complete contrast to Blubber's fluky, long-range blaster, requiring a great deal more technical skill.

The final whistle blew soon after that, putting an end to the Whalers' misery. The two captains shook hands as they left the pitch and Scott paid Rangers a sporting compliment. "We just couldn't live with your power once we changed ends," he admitted. "You're the best attacking team we've ever met."

"Great stuff, lads," Mr Thomas greeted them as they returned to the cabin. "If anybody's lost count of the score, we won 7–4."

"A remarkable turnabout," said Mr Stoppard, shaking his head in astonishment. "Talk about a game of two halves."

"Just like our double time slip," whispered Anil, who was sitting on a bench next to Worm in a corner of the room.

"Yeah, we were all at sea against the Vikings, but just managed to keep our heads above water," Worm giggled in reply as more puns came to mind. "Then it was plain sailing with the Scoresbys until Will was left hanging on by his fingertips."

Anil grinned. "I think we just about came out on top in the end, though. Won on aggregate."

Mr Stoppard was still speaking. "Just

goes to prove that it's a funny old game, as they say. Anything can happen in football."

"And on tour," Worm added under his breath. "I can't wait to find out who we'll meet on the next leg of our travels!"